Bicycling

Published by Creative Education

P.O. Box 227, Mankato, Minnesota 56002

Creative Education is an imprint of The Creative Company

Design and production by Blue Design, Portland, Maine

Printed in the United States of America

Photographs by Getty Images (Aurora, Al Bello, Hulton Archive, National Geographic, Photonica, Matt Turner)

Library of Congress Cataloging-in-Publication Data

Bodden, Valerie.

Bicycling / by Valerie Bodden.

p. cm. — (Active sports)

Includes index.

ISBN-13: 978-1-58341-467-5

1. Cycling—Juvenile literature. I. Title.

GV1043.5.B63 2007

796.6—dc22   2006018702

First Edition

9 8 7 6 5 4 3 2 1

Bicycling

Valerie Bodden

You feel the wind on your face. The sun shines on your back. You pedal faster and faster. There is nothing like riding a bike!

Riding a bike is good exercise and fun.

6. Renn-Bicycle „Invincible".

13. Humber-Tricycle.

8. Saal-Bicycle.

12. Sicherheits-Bicycle „Rover".

The first bikes were made out of wood.

10. Manuped.

11. Reitmaschine nach Freiherrn von Drais.

2. Tandem-Tricycle v Humber u. Comp.

Touren-Bicycle „Leipzig".

1. Touren-Tricycle „Invincible".

5. „Sociable" für 2 Perso verwandelbar in ein Tric

7. Gepäck-Tra port-Dreira

The first bikes were made a long time ago. They were slow. They did not have pedals! People pushed their feet against the ground to move.

Today, people ride all kinds of bikes. Some people ride bikes called touring bikes. Touring bikes are tall. They can go fast. People ride touring bikes on the road.

Many people in China like to ride bikes.

Some people ride mountain bikes. Mountain bikes are strong. People can ride them **off-road**. Mountain bikes can go over big bumps. They can go up and down mountains.

Some bikes are strong. Other bikes are fast.

Many kids ride small BMX bikes.

Lots of kids ride BMX bikes.
BMX bikes are small. But they
are strong. BMX bikes can go
off-road, too.

Some people ride bikes to get places. Kids ride them to school. Grown-ups ride them to work. Lots of people ride bikes for fun. Some people ride bikes in races.

Some woods have bike-riding trails.

There are lots of racers in the Tour de France.

Some people race touring bikes. The biggest race for touring bikes is called the Tour de France. The Tour de France is a long race. It takes three weeks! A biker named Lance Armstrong won the Tour de France seven times.

Lots of people race mountain bikes. Some people race them up hills. Others race them through **obstacles** (*OB-stuh-kuls*). Ned Overend was the **champion** of mountain bike racing four times.

Mountain bikes were first made about 30 years ago.

Lots of kids race BMX bikes. Most of the kids are 8 to 16 years old. BMX racers ride their bikes on dirt tracks. They have to go over jumps. John Tomac was a good BMX racer.

Some BMX bikers do tricks on bike ramps.

Some bike races go down mountains.

All bike racers need to stay safe. People who ride bikes just for fun need to stay safe, too. All bike riders should wear a helmet. It keeps them safe while they have fun!

GLOSSARY

champion—a person who wins first place in a race or sport

obstacles—things such as ditches and bumps that bikers ride through or over

off-road—off of the road, over dirt, grass, and rocks

tricks—special moves, such as riding with one wheel in the air

INDEX